E
MA

Mayer, Mercer

Frog on his own

$8.89

FROG
ON HIS OWN

by Mercer Mayer

DIAL BOOKS FOR YOUNG READERS
New York

For Father Yonov
and his family

Published by Dial Books for Young Readers
A division of E. P. Dutton | A division of New American Library
2 Park Avenue, New York, New York 10016
Library of Congress Catalog Card Number: 73-6017
Printed in Hong Kong by South China Printing Co.
COBE
8 10 12 14 15 13 11 9

PUT TRASH
HERE

PARK
DEPT.